THE LEGEND OF THE
Dogwood

Written by
BRENDA GOUGH

Illustrated by
MALINDA MAYS

The Overmountain Press
JOHNSON CITY, TENNESSEE

ISBN 13: 978-1-57072-321-6
ISBN 10: 1-57072-321-4
Copyright © 2008 by Brenda Gough
Printed in the United States of America
All Rights Reserved

1 2 3 4 5 6 7 8 9 0

Dedication

For the glory of my Heavenly Father
and in memory of my earthly father,
Carl B. Burnett, who first told me the
Legend of the Dogwood. I know they
dwell together.

–BG

To my Lord for the inspiration and
gift, and to the memory of my father,
Leon "Buster" Darnell, and my mother,
Ermie Tabers Darnell.

–MM

Foreword

The Legend of the Dogwood is a beautiful piece of Southern folklore. The Dogwood tree blooms at Easter. We do not know what wood was used to make the Cross of Christ, but this wonderful story reminds us of why we celebrate Easter.

The Dogwood tree stood tall and straight.
It was the greatest of all the trees in
the land. In the spring, its snowy white
blossoms could be seen from afar. A road
lay beneath the tree. Hundreds of people
followed the road to and from Jerusalem
each day. The tree pondered the different
sights it saw on the road.

Caravans of merchants passing.

Roman soldiers passing.

The rich and the poor passing.

Families passing.
The road was teeming with life.

The Dogwood's thoughts were interrupted by the sound of hooves carefully picking their way along the road. A young man was leading a donkey toward the tree. A woman cradling a sleeping baby boy in her arms rode on the back of the donkey. They were on their way to the temple in Jerusalem to present the child to God. They stopped under the tree. An unexplainable joy filled the Dogwood as it peered down at the infant. The Dogwood knew that it would never forget this child.

Twelve years later, the man and woman once again traveled to Jerusalem. With them was the boy. As the tree looked at the boy, the tree felt the same wondrous joy that it had felt before. The boy looked up at the Dogwood. His eyes were wise beyond His age. As the boy's gaze traveled up through the branches of the great tree, the Dogwood felt humbled to be in the presence of the child.

The years went by, and the tree saw the child from time to time. The Dogwood marveled at His growth and goodness. The boy grew to manhood. Other men followed Him. The man and His followers sometimes rested beneath the Dogwood tree. The man's voice was kind and full of love. His followers called him Jesus. The tree was glad to know His name. In the shade of the Dogwood's branches, Jesus spoke to His followers of love, forgiveness, and eternal life.

A quiet day burst into celebration with Jesus riding in the midst of a crowd. Men removed their cloaks and spread them on the ground before Him. The Dogwood was glad to see this wonderful man so honored. As Jesus passed, He looked up at the Dogwood. There was sadness in His eyes where only joy should be. The tree was confused. What could be wrong?

A detachment of Roman soldiers marched down
the road. They stopped beneath the Dogwood
and looked at its mighty trunk.

"Let us use this great Dogwood tree to crucify
Jesus," one of the soldiers gruffly said.

Another soldier answered, "It will make a perfect
cross for this man—who dares to call himself the
Son of God—to die upon."

Upon hearing these words, the Dogwood was
alarmed and frightened. It trembled in the wind
as it silently pleaded not to be used for such a
cruel purpose.

The soldiers took their axes and chopped the great tree down. As the Dogwood crashed to the ground, it moaned, "God have pity upon me."

The Dogwood tree was made into the Cross of Christ. As the nails pierced Jesus, they pierced the Cross. Jesus suffered and died on the Cross made from the Dogwood. People who loved Him carried His body away. For two days the world seemed dark. The Cross felt cold, sorrowful, and alone.

On the third day, the first rays of
the sun touched the empty Cross.
The Cross felt the warmth.

Suddenly, in the golden morning light,
Jesus stood looking up at the Cross.
    "Forgive me," whispered the Cross.
    Jesus felt compassion for the Cross
and forgave it for the part it had played
in His crucifixion.

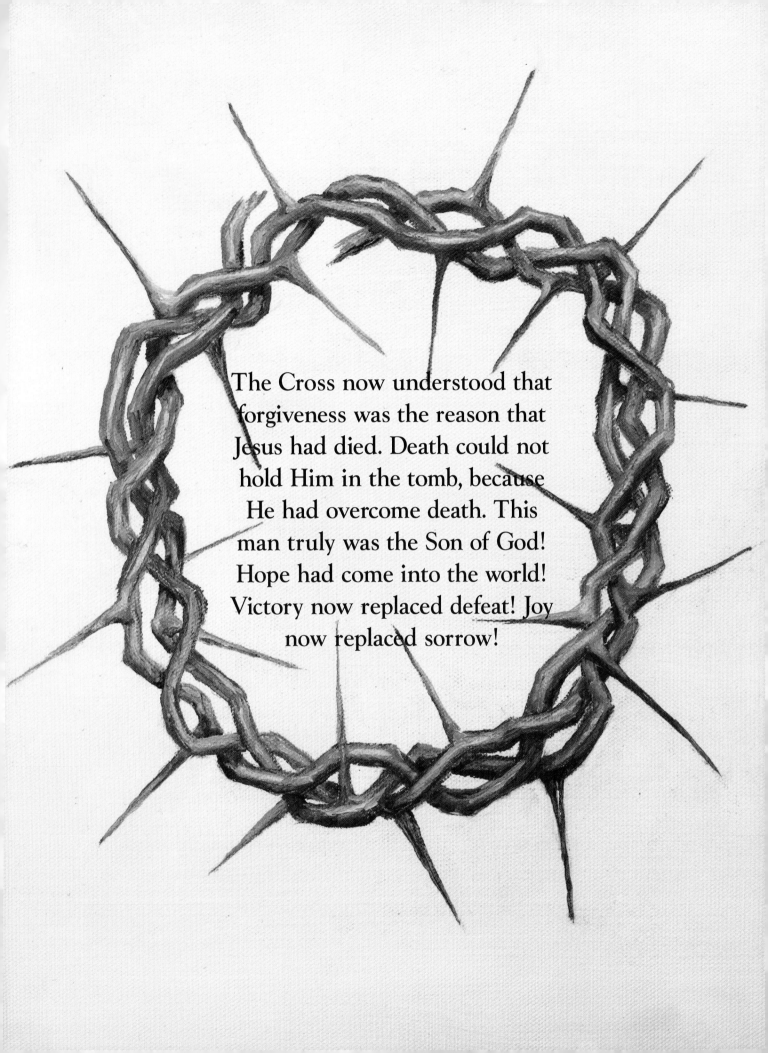

The Cross now understood that forgiveness was the reason that Jesus had died. Death could not hold Him in the tomb, because He had overcome death. This man truly was the Son of God! Hope had come into the world! Victory now replaced defeat! Joy now replaced sorrow!

From that day on, the Dogwood tree has never grown large enough to be made into a cross. The two long and two short petals of its blossoms form the cross; on the outer edge of each petal is a nail print, brown with rust and stained with red to represent the blood of Jesus. In the center of the flower grows a crown of thorns like the harsh crown mockingly placed on Jesus' head by the Roman soldiers.

In the spring, when dogwood blossoms unfold, all who see them remember Jesus' love and sacrifice. The dogwood tree is forever blessed. With its blooming comes the renewal of life.

Let the field be joyful, and all that is therein:
then shall all the trees of the wood rejoice

Psalm 96:12